THIS BOOK IS DEDICATED TO LUCA AND WILF

First published in Great Britain in 2013 by Simon and Schuster UK Ltd,
a CBS company.
Simon & Schuster UK Ltd
1st Floor, 222 Gray's Inn Road, London WC1X 8HB

www.simonandschuster.co.uk

Text copyright © Jack Carson 2013
With special thanks to Matt Whyman and Michelle Misra
Cover illustration copyright © Lorenzo Etherington 2013
Interior illustration copyright © Damien Jones 2013

The right of Jack Carson, Lorenzo Etherington and Damien Jones to be identified
as the author and illustrators of this work respectively has been asserted by them
in accordance with sections 77 and 78 of the Copyright,
Designs and Patents Act, 1988.

A CIP catalogue record for this book is available from the British Library.

PB ISBN: 978-0-85707-561-1
eBook ISBN: 978-0-85707-562-8

1 3 5 7 9 10 8 6 4 2

Printed and bound by
CPI Group (UK) Ltd, Croydon, CR0 4YY

BATTLE CHAMPIONS

CANYON CLASH

JACK CARSON

SIMON AND SCHUSTER

THE CHAMPIONSHIP TRAIL

Prairie Territory

The Canyon

Mines

Rust Town

adlands

Mines

OCEAN TERMINAL

Prologue

Sometime in the future, a war destroys the world as we know it. As people struggle to rebuild their lives, a new sport emerges from the ruins. In the Battle Championship, giant robots known as 'mechs' square up to one another and fight like gladiators. They're controlled from the inside by talented pilots, in a fight that tests man and machine to the limit.

All kids grow up dreaming of piloting a mech, and Titch Darwin is no exception. But for Titch it's personal. He is the son of one of the greatest Battle Champions – a man who went missing on the Championship trail – and the only way for Titch to find out what happened is to follow in his father's footsteps . . .

1

Rust Town

Under a blistering sun, Titch and his friend Martha made their way across the plain on horseback. They had been riding throughout the day – a long and tough journey – but finally the end was in sight.

'At last,' Titch declared, pushing back his mop of sandy hair as the old trading post, Rust Town, came into view before them. 'I'm looking forward to a bath and a decent bed for the night.'

'We can't rest straight away.' Martha jabbed a thumb over her shoulder as if to remind Titch of something. 'There's work to be done if we're going to be fighting fit for the first round of the

Battle Championship season!'

Titch glanced to where she was pointing and grinned. Close behind them towered a giant mech robot. Every footstep it took caused the ground to shudder. The machine was as high as a house, with two glowing red lights for eyes and a cockpit embedded in its chest. Titch who was a small boy for his age, craned his neck for a better look. Through the reinforced glass, he could just about see the pilot inside.

'Hey, Finn!' he called, speaking into a microphone clipped to his collar. 'How's it going in there?'

'I'm cool!' came the reply into his earpiece. 'Mostly because Martha fixed the fan unit before we set off!'

Martha chuckled and shook her head. She was a kind-looking girl, with sharp cheekbones and almond-shaped eyes. As the mechanic, it was her job to make sure

the mech was fully operational. Her twin brother Finn served as the test pilot, while Titch would take over for the Championship battle rounds. The three friends had only just graduated from Mech Academy, so they were still feeling pretty nervous. Even so, after months of hard training, they were excited about finally having the chance to compete.

'Do you think Alexei will be there yet?' asked Finn over the mech's radio system...

'I hope not,' groaned Titch, thinking

about the blond-haired boy who'd graduated with them from Mech Academy. They hadn't exactly hit it off. In fact, they were more like arch-enemies as Alexei was often quick to cheat and even sabotage Titch's chances.

'Let's not think about Alexei now,' said Titch, trying to put the boy out of his mind. 'We've got more important things to worry about,' he added, glancing at the town before them. It stood at the mouth of a huge canyon which looked like a vast and jagged crack in a rocky plain.

'One thing's for sure – you'll have to watch out for attacks from above,' said Martha, her gaze locked on the landscape behind the town. 'That's quite a battle zone!'

Titch could see that for himself. The canyon was enormous! And this weekend, it would host the Battle Championship. Already, grandstands had been erected at the top. At first light tomorrow morning, they would be full of spectators. Then, down below on the canyon floor, the fighting would begin in knockout rounds.

'If I stand any chance of getting through all three rounds,' said Titch, 'I'm going to need eyes in the back of my head!'

'That's where your mech's on-board computer comes in,' chuckled Finn through the headset. 'Remember – the radar screen will stop you from being taken by surprise. It's your reaction times that matter. If you come under attack and move too slowly, Martha and I can expect to be picking up cogs and gearwheels until sundown.'

Titch smiled at the thought as he steered his horse towards the town. That so wasn't going to happen if he could help it.

He looked about him. Rust Town was a dusty, rough-looking place. Most of the people who came here were just passing through on horseback – from gold hunters

to ranch hands. Some of the other Battle Championship competitors had clearly already arrived by the look of the mechs striding down the main street. From a distance, they seemed like giants moving among humans.

Titch watched as one of the mechs stopped outside the town's scavenger store. This was where competitors could pick up parts and weapons for their fighting machines. A set of automatic

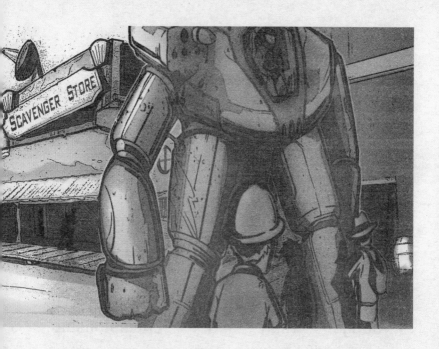

steps unfolded from the mech's chest. Then the pilot climbed out from the cockpit and made his way inside. Titch hoped the store was well stocked. They had yet to arm their own mech after all.

'First thing we need to do is check in with the officials,' said Martha, as they drew their horses to a halt just inside the main gates.

'That's where we need to go.' Titch pointed, drawing their attention to a

Battle Championship banner that was strung across the far end of the street. He guided his horse towards it and Martha and Finn followed in a line. Chickens scratched at the dirt in front of them, only to hurry away when they saw the approaching mech. Next, they passed the saloon bar. From inside, brooding cowboys stared back, Titch tried not to look at them. He and his two friends were much younger than most Championship contenders. They were the new generation of fighters. Titch had proven himself to be bold, brave and lightning quick but just then, he simply felt like a new boy on his first day at school. The last thing he wanted was trouble . . .

•

'Name?' asked a gruff man with a clipboard, as the three of them arrived at a table outside the competitors' area. He had already demanded that they produce their licences that allowed them to pilot a mech.

'Titch. Titch Darwin.'

The man sighed and narrowed his eyes. 'Not you,' he said. 'Your mech. What name are you fighting under?'

'Oh.' Titch turned to Martha in surprise. At the same time, Finn climbed down the steps from the cockpit. He shared the same features as his sister, but his kind smile faded as he considered the question.

'We haven't got a name,' whispered Martha. 'Every other mech has a fighting name, like Sidewinder and Scar. What do we call ourselves?'

'How about Ronald?' Finn suggested.

Titch and Martha exchanged a baffled glance.

'Finn, that's the worst name ever! You can't call a mech Ronald! Everyone will laugh at us.'

Finn shrugged. 'It was the name of our family dog.'

'Finn,' said Martha, 'This mech is a lean, mean fighting machine! Ronald was even scared of cats! We can do much better than that!'

The man at the table sighed and looked at his watch. 'No name, no entry,' he told them.

Martha looked at Titch. 'So what was your dad's mech called?' she asked.

Many years earlier, when Titch was just a baby, his father had set out on the Battle Championship trail. After several seasons, he had disappeared mysteriously. Titch was determined to find out what had happened to him – it was one of the reasons he'd gone to Mech Academy himself. All he knew was that his dad had been a shining star of the sport. Everything else remained a mystery.

'I'm afraid I don't know the name of

his mech,' he said glumly. Then he glanced back at his machine, and an idea entered his head. 'I know it doesn't sound like much, but I have a name in mind.'

'What's that?' asked Martha.

'In honour of the brains behind that metal brawn,' said Titch, 'let's name it after the on-board computer!'

'LoneStar?' Martha seemed surprised, only to grin when she realised Titch was being deadly serious. 'The perfect name,' she said, and turned to the man with the clipboard. 'Our mech is called LoneStar.'

With the registration form folded safely inside his pocket, Titch and the twins moved their freshly-named mech into a fenced-off area where Battle Championship crews were working on their machines. They could've been looking at metal statues of muscle-bound gladiators. Each mech had been customised in different ways, but all of them had one

thing in common — they bristled with weapons. Titch's mech just didn't compare. It had only been used for training purposes back at Mech Academy, but Titch had formed a bond with it, and taken it with him. LoneStar was big, but these state-of-the-art contenders overshadowed Titch's machine in every way.

'This is the Armoury,' said Martha, looking around. 'I'm going to be spending some time in here making sure our mech is fit to fight tomorrow.'

'It isn't a bit like the Mech Academy,' whispered Finn.

'Welcome to the real world,' his sister told him, as she opened up her toolbox. 'Now I need to carry out some updates on the defence sensors. Why don't you guys visit the scavenger store? Look for any mech accessory that might give us an advantage in canyon battle conditions.'

'First on our shopping list should be a

pair of super-spring knee joints,' joked Finn in a bid to lighten the mood. 'Let's face it, judging by some of the machines in here, it looks like Titch will need a mech that's equipped to run away!'

• • •

2

Choosing Weapons

The scavenger store wasn't a welcoming place to visit. As Titch and Finn looked around them, an uncomfortable hush filled the air. A bare light bulb lit the room, and sawdust was scattered across the floor. Titch and Finn took a moment for their eyes to adjust to the gloom.

'What can I do for you, kids?' The storekeeper appeared at the counter. She was a fierce-looking woman with wild black hair and a patch over one eye. 'You'd better not be here just to browse. I'm running a business.'

'We know,' said Titch, letting out a sigh as he looked around him. The store was jam-packed with mech parts, from boxes of tiny gearwheels to huge steel backbones stored on brackets high up the walls. Titch peered at the jumble of parts. He didn't know where to begin!

'Our mech is unarmed right now,' he told the storekeeper. 'We need to get it battle-ready.'

'OK, so who are you fighting tomorrow?' she asked.

Titch and Finn turned to one another, and then shrugged. 'We don't know,' they said in unison.

'This is our first season,' Titch went on to explain. 'We're new to the game.'

The storekeeper switched her good eye from Titch to Finn and back again. 'The Battle Championship always needs fresh blood. Just be aware that most newbies find it tough for quite a while. Some of the contenders out there have been fighting for years.'

'We know that,' said Finn. 'It's why we want some weapons that won't let us down.'

'Then it's lucky you came here,' she said, turning to a battered computer on a desk behind her. She tapped at the keyboard and then peered at the screen. 'What's your mech called?'

'LoneStar,' said Titch.

They watched as the woman scrolled through the list of competitors. Finally, she stopped. 'Oh, now that's just bad luck,' she muttered to herself.

'What's the matter?' asked Titch.

'Nothing!' The storekeeper returned to the counter once again. She smiled weakly. 'OK. The fact is you've been drawn to fight against Eagle Slam in the first round,' she confessed. 'That mech will use the height of the canyon to its advantage. It'll scale the walls and stay out of sight. So, when it attacks, you literally won't know what's hit you until it's too late.'

All of a sudden, both boys looked worried.

'So what weapons should we bolt on to our mech?' Titch paused and cleared his throat. 'Is there anything that can help us? There must be something we can do to avoid certain defeat?'

The storekeeper tapped her fingers on the counter for a moment.

'Very well,' she said. 'If you're brave enough to face Eagle Slam, then I guess you're going to need a FlingNet.'

'What's that?' asked Finn.

'It's your only chance of winning.' The woman reached for a pad of paper. 'A test fire will show you how the weapon works. I can arrange to have it delivered to the Armoury within the hour. Now I'm guessing that as well as the FlingNet, you'll want to fit your mech with some kind of assault rifle, right? A NailStormer would work well.'

'Anything that might stop a mech in

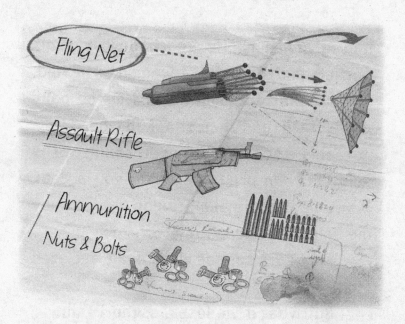

its tracks,' said Titch. 'There are some tight spots in that canyon. I need to be sure that one hit will do some damage.'

The storekeeper scribbled out a list. She then tore off the top sheet and offered it to the boys. Titch stepped forward to take it, only for her to snatch it back.

'You can't just have these weapons for free,' she said. 'Either you trade in your old stuff, or pay me.'

Titch had some money that his mother

had given him. He reached inside his pockets and showed the woman all he had. She picked through the coins in the palm of his hand, and then shook her head.

'This won't even buy you a bullet,' she said. 'But I'm prepared to do you a deal. If you beat Eagle Slam tomorrow, you pay me half the prize money.'

'That sure sounds like a deal!' declared Finn.

'But what if we lose?' asked Titch.

The storekeeper's expression darkened.

'If Eagle Slam defeats you,' she warned, 'I'll take your mech as payment and break it up for spare parts.'

•

Later that day, Titch stood nervously at the foot of the steps to his mech. Martha had just finished fitting the machine with the weapons delivered from the scavenger store. She returned a wrench to her toolbox and then wiped the oil from her hands with a rag.

'It's taken much longer than I expected,' she said, 'but at last we're battle-ready!'

The sun was setting over Rust Town. Behind the Armoury, in the canyon, mechs could be heard trying out their weapons. It was official practice time for the Battle Championship competitors – a chance for the pilots to get comfortable with their machines and make sure they'd picked the right firepower. While Martha struggled to fit the FlingNet, Finn had gone off to take a sneak peek at the other competitors. Just as Titch prepared to climb into the cockpit, Finn returned, looking worried.

'The storekeeper was right about Eagle Slam,' he said. 'It's an awesome machine.'

'What can it do?' asked Titch.

'Get yourself into the canyon and see for yourself,' replied Finn.

•

Minutes later, Titch found himself steering his mech between giant walls of rock. By now the sun was so low that the canyon was cast in shadow. Strapped inside the cockpit, he frowned and punched a button.

'Hey, LoneStar,' he said, addressing the on-board computer. 'Can you switch the camera to night vision?'

'Coming right up,' replied a tinny voice from a loudspeaker. 'My sensors report that the canyon is crawling with mechs trying out their weapons. Titch, it's time to get battle-ready!'

The camera was mounted on the mech's head. Titch was wearing a special helmet with sensors attached and a projector inside the visor. It meant that when he looked around, the mech's head would do the same thing and allow Titch to view his surroundings.

Just then, as he peered around the canyon floor, the camera's night vision revealed another mech. This one looked strikingly different from his own. It crawled by on four pincer-style limbs, sporting snapping claws at the front and a huge steel tail curled right over the machine's head.

'It looks like some kind of giant insect,' said Titch.

'Agreed,' replied LoneStar, 'but then we're not drawn against Scorpion in the first round. We need to focus on doing our best against Eagle Slam.'

'Bring it on,' said Titch, preparing to try out his own weapons. The FlingNet was attached to one arm. On the other was the NailStormer gun that the woman from the scavenger store had supplied. It had been Titch's favoured weapon back at the Academy, and spewed explosive steel darts that were sure to bring a mech down. That was if Titch could find it in his sights.

'Practice time is running out,' LoneStar

reminded him. 'Time to try out the FlingNet.'

Titch guided the mech onwards until he came across a boulder. It would serve as the perfect target for his first attempt. Carefully, he raised the mech's arm. A target appeared on the screen. Titch locked it on to the boulder, found the fire button on top of the control stick and then pressed it with his thumb. The weapon fired with a gigantic snapping sound, which took Titch by surprise. Such was the force of the shot that the mech stumbled backwards with its arms flailing. As a result, the net inside the gun's barrel soared high into the air, opened wide and then floated back down to cloak Titch's mech.

'I might need to try that again,' said Titch as he peered through the mesh that now covered LoneStar. 'Hopefully nobody was watching!'

As he prepared to claw off the net, something drew his attention upwards.

With an ear-splitting shriek, a huge mech appeared to tip from a ledge high up in the canyon. At first, Titch thought it was falling, but then he saw the machine spread its arms and a pair of steel wings fanned out. In awe, Titch watched the mech sail across the canyon, towards a rocky outcrop on the other side. Midway across, the mech circled round. With its hooked beak and talons, it looked like a monstrous bird of prey made from metal. Titch had no doubt who he was looking at. The name left his lips in a whisper.

'Eagle Slam,' he breathed.

'So that's our opponent tomorrow,' said LoneStar. 'I'm not programmed to have feelings, so it must be a malfunction, but my status monitor reports that my knees have started knocking!'

● ● ●

3

Into Battle!

Titch slept badly that night. It didn't help that his room above the saloon bar overlooked Rust Town's main street. Every now and then, an argument or fist fight would break out between cowboys. It was a rough, tough place to be. All that Titch could do was remind himself that he was following a dream. Only the best were selected to fight in the Battle Championship. Just being here, preparing for the first knockout round, would've made his father proud.

'I'll put my heart and soul into this fight,' he said, staring at the ceiling while thinking about his dad. 'If only you were here to watch me.'

At first light, Martha and Finn found Titch waiting for them in the Armoury. The place was humming with activity. Already some of the pilots had climbed inside their mechs. As soon as the twins arrived, Titch drew their attention to one team in particular.

'Check out Eagle Slam,' he said, pointing at the bird-like mech. Instead of standing tall, like all the other machines, it was perched on a girder. The pilot and his crew were standing underneath it, using the machine as shade from the sun. They were huddled close together, clearly talking through tactics. All of them looked like they'd taken part in many seasons of the Battle Championship.

'Just do what you can.' Finn clapped Titch on the shoulder. 'You're a talented pilot. One of the best the Academy had ever seen, remember?'

As the three friends made their final preparations, the Championship officials addressed the mech crews over a loudspeaker system. Everyone went quiet.

'The first battle will start in ten minutes,' the tannoy announced. 'Would Eagle Slam and LoneStar please make their way into the canyon!'

Martha smiled bravely at Titch. 'Are you ready?' she asked.

'As ready as I'll ever be,' he answered her, watching as the pilot climbed into Eagle Slam's cockpit. A moment later, the bird-like mech stretched its metal wings wide and shrieked. It was an alarming sound, amplified by speakers set on each side of the machine's hooked beak.

'It's just a recording,' Martha assured him. 'I expect they're just trying to unsettle you, but you look good to me, Titch.'

'All systems are ready,' he said, trying

hard not to let them see that he was worried.

As Titch steered his mech into the canyon, he looked about him. The grandstands on both sides were packed. The cheers sounded muffled from inside the cockpit, as did the chanting for his opponent. Eagle Slam had already taken up position. The machine faced Titch's mech. It was some distance away, with its wings tucked tight and both eyes gleaming.

'Eagle Slam is a three times Battle Champion,' warned LoneStar. 'But hey, you're a new boy in his first season! Nobody's expecting much from you.'

'Thanks for that,' muttered Titch as he brought the mech to a halt, facing his opponent. 'You're a big help.'

'Here to serve,' replied his on-board computer. 'Now, do you have any last requests?'

'Just one,' said Titch. 'Please stop

talking and let's focus on the fight!'

Through his earpiece just then, the referee began a countdown from ten. Titch glanced at the control panels. Everything was functioning properly.

'3 ... 2 ... 1. Let battle commence!'

Before Titch could even blink, his opponent had opened its wings and was pushing up on both legs. He watched as the monstrous mech rose up into the air, powered by the rockets underneath its steel tail feathers, and then swooped towards him. Titch responded with a burst of fire from his NailStormer.

'Take that!' he yelled, as a flurry of steel darts streaked towards the target. Each one connected with the soaring mech's undercarriage and exploded on impact. Titch was so thrilled to have made the first move that he just kept his finger on the trigger.

Such an intense attack created a

fireball around his opponent. At first, Titch thought he must have brought the mech down. But just as he was starting to relax, two huge metal talons burst out of the smoke. With a terrible jolt, Titch felt his mech being hoisted into the air.

'Outside sensors report that we've been grabbed by the shoulder rungs,' said LoneStar.

As Eagle Slam carried its prey away, the canyon floor appeared to shrink and turn on Titch's screen.

'If he takes us any higher, we'll never survive the drop!' cried Titch, wrestling with his control sticks in a frantic bid to shake the mech free.

'You have one more round of NailStormer darts,' reported LoneStar. 'Use them wisely.'

Immediately, Titch armed the weapon and aimed it upwards. Quickly, he released the last of the darts into his opponent.

This time, it caused Eagle Slam to cry out. The machine continued to pump the air with its wings, but was clearly struggling. Titch seized the advantage. Using both his mech's arms, he reached up, grabbed Eagle Slam by the leg and began to twist around.

'That mech can't hold on to us for much longer!' said LoneStar, as their opponent fought to stay in the air. 'We're hurting him bad!'

The drop, when it happened, took both Titch and the crowd by surprise. As soon as Eagle Slam opened up its talons, every alarm inside the cockpit began to sound.

•

'We're falling!' Titch cried over the din. There was nothing he could do but adopt the crash position. With a sickening crunch, LoneStar hit the ground. The impact took Titch's breath away. It also caused several instrument panels to crash across the cockpit. A second later, Titch dared to open his eyes. An alarm was still ringing. Wires and cables were hanging everywhere and a strong smell of burning filled his nostrils. 'Talk to me, LoneStar!' he said. 'Are you with me?'

'For as long as the power pack lasts,' replied the on-board computer, sounding somewhat distorted through a broken

speaker. 'But I should warn you that Eagle Slam is preparing to finish us off!'

Titch looked up. The camera showed his opponent was wheeling around in the sky with wings outstretched. With LoneStar sprawled on its back, Titch grabbed the control sticks and tried to roll out of the way, but the machine simply juddered and failed to move.

As he pulled and jabbed harder, Eagle Slam tipped into a dive. In a panic, Titch hoisted the NailStormer high and pulled the trigger. The weapon's barrel simply clicked. It was all out of darts. With no time to think, Titch switched to the FlingNet. With his opponent dropping out of the sky towards him, he couldn't afford to get it wrong. This time, he braced his mech for the kickback when he fired the weapon. With a snap, the net shot upwards and opened wide.

'Please work,' Titch whispered to

himself, and gasped as the net connected with the target. 'Yes!' he cried as it tangled around Eagle Slam. The flying mech screeched in surprise this time. It spiralled around, struggling to free itself while plunging to the ground.

'We need to move!' LoneStar informed Titch. 'Otherwise we're going to be squashed!'

Once again, Titch tried and failed to roll the mech clear. The motor system simply coughed. But he wasn't going to give up. With his opponent just seconds from crashing, he made one more attempt. The mech juddered, and then snapped to one side as the motor came alive. At the same time, Eagle Slam hit the ground where LoneStar had been lying. The machine came down with such a crunch that it left the spectators in silence. Titch should have been overjoyed. Instead, his concern turned to the pilot inside.

'We need to get him out of there!' he cried, unharnessing his seat belt. 'Drop the steps for me, LoneStar. Quick!'

His concern didn't last long. As he began to scramble up the smoking remains of Eagle Slam, the cockpit panel popped open and a figure staggered out. The pilot rested his hands on his knees for a moment, as if to get his breath back. Titch paused, wondering if he might be in trouble for wrecking such a legendary mech. The pilot stood upright, and fixed Titch in his sights. Then, to a roar from the grandstands above, he saluted the boy who had beaten him.

● ● ●

4
Emergency Repairs

All the way back to the Armoury, LoneStar announced the long list of damage that Titch's mech had suffered.

'Is there anything that isn't broken?' Titch asked, as he steered the machine out of the canyon. Afraid that LoneStar might just break down completely, he moved the control sticks as gently as possible.

'We're in a bad way,' said the on-board computer, 'but don't let that spoil your victory!'

At the mouth of the canyon, Titch stepped aside to let the recovery truck pass. Eagle Slam had been hooked up to the back by a series of chains. Titch watched the vehicle drag it out through the dust. The officials waved him on, keen to clear the canyon for the next battle in this first round. Then he spotted Martha and Finn waiting for him.

'I still can't believe that we won!' Titch said, racing down the steps and into their arms. 'We did it. A great team effort, guys!'

'You're through to round two!' cried Finn.

'No,' said Titch. 'We're through to round two! I couldn't have done it without you guys!'

'It's a great result,' added Martha.

'A lucky result more like!' a voice came from behind them.

Titch spun round to see another pilot – a pilot he instantly recognised.

'Alexei!' Titch groaned. He'd been wondering when they'd run into him.

'That wasn't just luck, Alexei,' said Martha. 'What Titch did out there took

more skill and guts than you've ever shown.'

'Well, we'll see about that,' Alexei grinned and turned his attention to LoneStar. 'Anyway, there's no way you'll get your mech fixed in time for the next round.'

'Really? Are you quite sure about that? We have until tomorrow morning,' replied Finn. 'My sister will work through the night if she has to.'

'Then don't let me stop you,' said Alexei. 'I'm off to prepare for my first fight. I'm up against a mech that looks even more clapped-out than yours. Winning won't be a problem for me! I'm sure to be joining you in the next round.'

Titch shook his head as Alexei left them.

'If he's planning on breaking the rules here,' he said, thinking about what Alexei had been like at Mech Academy, 'chances are he'll be disqualified and sent home straight away.'

'Let's not worry about him,' said Martha. Quietly, she turned once more to look up at their mech.

LoneStar towered over them, looking somewhat sorry for itself. A little smoke was twisting from a shoulder joint, while a cluster of exposed wires at one knee kept spitting out sparks.

'I'll download the damage report from LoneStar,' Martha continued, 'and then we'd better get ourselves to the scavenger store straight away. We're going to need a lot of spare parts!'

•

When the three friends entered the store, the owner was pleased to see them.
'Well, well, here comes the surprise victor – a nice little earner for a first match,' she said. 'So half belongs to me, just as we agreed, and as for your share . . . well, that

won't even cover the replacement parts. The only way you can pay for it all is by selling back your weapons.'

Titch looked at the twins. 'An unarmed mech is better than no mech at all,' he said.

'But what about tomorrow's fight?' asked Finn.

'Let's get the mech fixed first. Then we'll worry about entering a battle round without weapons.'

Martha and Finn both nodded reluctantly.

'OK, so here's the list,' said Martha, and presented a long printout of what she'd need.

The storekeeper took a moment to read through to the end.

'I can have everything you want delivered to the Armoury right away,' she said, much to their relief. Then she frowned and tutted. Titch held his breath.

'Everything except the energy acceleration unit.'

'Oh, no!' groaned Martha.

Finn and Titch exchanged a worried glance. Then they looked to the storekeeper for some kind of explanation.

'Without the unit, your mech will have the reaction times of a tortoise,' she told them. 'You'd lose the next round within seconds.'

'So what can we do?' asked Finn. 'If Titch can't even make his mech run away quickly, then we might as well pack up right now.'

Martha frowned at her twin brother.

'Titch isn't the kind of Battle Championship contender who runs away,' she reminded him. 'He's a fighter. It's in his blood. If we can repair the mech, I know Titch will put his heart and soul into tomorrow's fight!'

The storekeeper listened to Martha

while looking at Titch intently. 'There's a scavenger store in the next town on the trail,' she told them. 'You might find an energy acceleration unit there, but it can only be fitted by their engineers.'

'I can fix everything else first,' Martha said to the boys. 'Then we should head off.'

'There's no time to lose,' added the storekeeper. 'That's if you want to make it back in time for tomorrow's Battle Championship round. Just be aware that it's a long ride through the canyons!'

'Thanks for your help,' said Titch, and turned with the others to leave. 'Let's hurry. There's no way I'm giving up now!'

•

Martha worked harder than Titch would have thought possible to repair the damaged mech. There was no time to rest when she finished. As soon as she closed her toolbox, Finn scrambled into the cockpit, while Titch waited with the horses.

'We'll have to ride without stopping,' he said.

'Then let's hit the trail!' replied Martha, and set off behind the mech. 'LoneStar will take some time to get there, but at least he's moving.'

Slowly, the three friends followed a track that took them up the canyon and behind the grandstands. Another one of the first-round fights was taking place. The clash of metal and explosions of every kind could be heard from the canyon below.

'It sounds like a mech is taking quite a beating,' said Titch, who heard Finn chuckle into his earpiece.

'Let's hope it's Alexei!' said the test pilot from the cockpit of LoneStar. 'One day he'll learn his lesson!'

•

By the time Titch, Finn and Martha arrived in the next town, dusk was beginning to settle. Luckily for them, the scavenger store was still open. And to their delight, the part they needed fitting was in stock.

'I haven't been asked for one of these in years,' said the engineer in charge of fitting the energy acceleration unit they needed. 'Normally, these units last forever, but once they're broken, they really need replacing. Anyway, let's just hope this one doesn't bring you bad luck.'

'Eh?' said Titch, confused.

'The last mech who needed a new unit like this went missing along with his pilot some days later,' the engineer explained. 'It was a real shame. He was one of the best the Battle Championship has seen.'

Titch looked shocked. It sounded like the man could be alking about his dad.

'Did he say anything to you before he left?' Titch asked.

The engineer shrugged as if he couldn't offer him anything further.

'It was a long time ago,' he said. 'Although I do remember he was nervous. The pilot kept looking over his shoulder while I worked.' He stopped and glanced at LoneStar. 'His mech was about as badly beaten up as this one.'

'Is there nothing else you can tell me about him?' said Titch, desperate to make the most of this first vital clue. 'It would mean a lot to me.'

The mechanic glanced at Titch's friends. It was clear to them that there was nothing more he could say to help.

'Leave it, Titch,' said Finn, and placed a hand on his friend's shoulder. 'It's enough to know for now that you're on the right track. Let the man get on with his work.'

Titch sighed to himself, but nodded all the same. As he watched the mechanic climb a ladder to fit the unit inside LoneStar, it felt like just the kind of good luck sign that he needed.

An hour later, Titch and Martha were climbing back on to their horses, waiting for Finn to fire up the mech. By now, stars glittered in the night sky. A full moon cast the landscape in a pale light. It was certainly bright enough to guide them on their return journey, but unfortunately, as LoneStar informed Finn, they wouldn't be able to do so until daybreak.

'No Battle Championship mech is allowed to set out across the trail after dark,' he told them, having hurried down the steps to share the bad news. 'The on-board computer is programmed to shut down one hour after sunset,' he explained. 'Apparently, the officials say it's just too dangerous to travel at night. It's when thieves, smugglers and mech rustlers stalk the trail!'

'LoneStar might've warned us earlier!' moaned Martha.

All of a sudden, Finn looked very sheepish.

'Actually, it did tell me on the way over. I thought it was the computer's idea of a bad joke.'

'Computers aren't supposed to joke,' said Martha crossly. 'This could cost us the chance of entering the next round. Maybe I need to take a good look at LoneStar's logic processor. He might have a screw loose.'

'Guys, let's not fall out over this,' said Titch, stepping between the twins. 'LoneStar has been good to me so far. He might be a little different from most on-board computers, but I'm sure we'll make it back in time. We'll just have to leave at the crack of dawn.' Titch returned to his horse and unbuckled the saddlebags. They contained everything they needed to make camp for the night. 'Let's get some sleep. It's been a long day after all.'

As he opened up the bags, a coyote started howling out on the prairie. Martha looked very unsettled.

'Sounds like it might be a long night, too,' she said.

• • •

5

No Time To Lose!

The three friends settled down under the stars. They built a campfire, just outside the gates of the town, and cooked beans in a pan. Then, when the flames had turned to glowing embers, they bedded down and went to sleep. Titch was exhausted after such a long day, but even he woke up with a start when a distant boom filled the air.

'What was that?' he whispered, as Martha and Finn rubbed their eyes and looked around.

'It sounded like dynamite!' said Finn.

'There are lots of gold and diamond mines in the canyons,' said Martha, snuggling back under her blanket. 'Let's hope whoever's behind it knows what they're doing. They might be hoping to get rich quick, but it can make the rocks unstable.'

'Really?' Finn sounded worried. 'The last thing we want to find tomorrow is that our path back has been blocked by boulders!'

'We'll find a way,' said Titch, and closed his eyes once more. 'That kind of obstacle won't stop our mech.'

•

The next time they woke, the sun was peeping over the horizon at daybreak. Within moments, LoneStar powered up and dropped the steps into place. By the time the first golden bars pushed across the prairie, Titch, Finn and Martha were on their way.

They didn't once stop to rest, with no time to spare before the second knockout round. This time they followed a different route. According to the mech's on-board computer, it would get them to Rust Town faster. The path took them through a winding canyon, with mile-high walls dotted with fossils. They even passed a party of young Battle Championship fans who had decided to explore the area.

'Wow!' said one, as the great mech halted before them. 'Is this for real?'

'It sure is,' said Titch, and climbed off

his horse alongside Martha. 'We're on our way to the first-round fight right now.'

'Is the path clear?' asked Finn, who had climbed out of the cockpit on to the platform. He sighed in relief when the leader of the group assured him they had come across no rockfall. 'Though you guys should be careful,' he added. 'We heard dynamite going off last night.'

'The only noise we've heard has been

65

the clash of fighting mechs,' said the group leader. 'We're taking a break to look around before heading back for the second round.'

Martha glanced at her watch.

'OK, let's roll,' she said, addressing Finn and Titch. 'If we miss the first round, that's our Championship weekend over.'

•

An hour later, when they finally reached the canyon where the fighting took place, one of the Battle Championship pilots was just climbing from the battered remains of his machine. Another mech towered over the toppled contender. It raised both fists, much to the delight of the crowd. As Titch watched the victory celebration, Finn left the cockpit to join them at ground level.

'Your round is next,' he said. 'LoneStar has just been instructed to take up position!'

Just then, the crowd erupted in

applause. The three friends turned to see the defeated machine being dragged away by the recovery truck. The winner followed close behind, but something else grabbed Titch's attention. The next contender had just arrived in the canyon. This mech had broad chrome shoulders and long cables sprouting from its scalp. It looked as wild as it did powerful, and was clutching a huge axe in each hand.

'I recognise that mech,' said Finn. 'It won the Championship last year. All without losing a single round!'

'It's Tomahawk!' his sister declared. 'The mech with the deadliest aim of all!'

Titch watched as his opponent showed off to the crowd by spinning each axe in his hands.

'How am I going to take on a mech like that when I've got no weapons?' he asked with a gasp.

Finn clapped Titch reassuringly on the

back. 'All you can do is rely on your wits,' he said. 'It's going to be a battle of brain over brawn!'

Once inside the cockpit, Titch broke the news to LoneStar.

'Without weapons, we're doomed!' replied the on-board computer. 'Tomahawk uses axes that carry an electrical charge. If one connects with the mech, it'll knock out the power system faster than the flick of a switch!'

'Well, we're not going to give up without a fight,' said Titch, positioning the mech for the start of the round. 'I have an idea.'

'Is it a good one?' asked LoneStar.

'We won't find out unless we try it!' said Titch, just as the countdown began for the start of the round.

•

The fight began with a well-aimed first throw from Tomahawk. Titch managed to steer LoneStar from the path of the flying

axe, but it left him off guard. All he could do was throw his machine into the dust when the second axe whizzed towards them.

'This is hopeless,' reported LoneStar. 'We're sitting ducks!'

Titch pulled back on the control sticks, lifting the mech back on to his feet. At the same time, Tomahawk rushed around him to collect the two axes. Titch backed away, preparing for the next assault.

'This time,' he told the on-board computer, as the camera showed his opponent lining up the next throw, 'we're going to hold steady.'

'That's the spirit!' said LoneStar.

'Now magnify the camera image. I need to track that axe when it comes at us.'

Immediately, the image on the screen closed in on the weapon. At the same time, Tomahawk lifted his axe high and hurled it at LoneStar.

'Here it comes!' said LoneStar, who locked the camera on the spinning axe. To help, the on-board computer even added data about its speed and closing distance. Titch tightened his grip on the control sticks.

'Nice and steady,' he said to himself, before flinging LoneStar's hand into the path of the flying axe. The handle connected with the machine's metal palm, which Titch quickly curled into a fist to catch the axe. 'And now we have a weapon!' he crowed.

Tomahawk growled, before hurling his second axe. It was clear that the pilot inside had been taken by surprise by Titch's quick action because the throw went wide. Now Titch had the advantage. With the target locked on Tomahawk, who suddenly looked very nervous, Titch prepared to make his one throw count. Even before he hurled it, he felt sure that the weapon would hit its target dead on.

Boom!

Titch could barely believe he had won his second round so swiftly. It was a result that went beyond his wildest dreams. Most importantly of all, it meant he'd be fighting in the final battle that afternoon!

'I just got lucky,' he told Martha back in the Armoury.

'You went in without weapons and came out with a win!' she reminded him. 'There's nothing lucky about what you did. That takes skill.'

'People are beginning to notice you,' Finn joined in. 'Look around!'

Titch glanced about. Sure enough, many of the mech crews had stopped work on their machines to watch Titch's return from the battleground. One pilot even crossed to congratulate him. When he took off his helmet and goggles, Titch was surprised to see it was Alexei.

'I lost my round earlier today,' he told

Titch, looking very disappointed indeed. 'So that's my weekend finished with only a few points on the leader board to show for it. But I'll only come back stronger at the next destination on the Championship calendar. Anyway, you should've seen the size of the mech I was up against earlier!' he added, and cast Martha a mean smile. 'It made Tomahawk look like a little girl!'

'Hey!' snapped Martha, who didn't take kindly to that sort of talk.

'Show some respect, Alexei,' said Titch. 'Without Martha, I wouldn't have stood a chance of winning. She's one of a kind.'

Alexei raised his hands, pretending to surrender. 'OK! OK!' he said. 'But it doesn't matter how good she is as a mechanic, this afternoon's final round is going to be your biggest test yet. You'd better be prepared, because whatever mech you're up against it's bound to be a beast of a machine!'

'We'll be fully prepared.' Martha looked over to where Finn was watching another team prep their mech. 'Between us we'll make sure LoneStar is fighting fit!'

•

With a few hours to go before the final round, the three friends worked hard to get ready. Martha headed for the scavenger store to try and strike another deal with the storekeeper. It was risky, because if they were defeated, they would lose their mech. Then again, it was the only way they could afford weapons. Titch agreed that they had no choice, but he was really feeling the pressure. To help him stay focused, Finn got him to stay behind with LoneStar and practise some moves. First they went through attack and defence positions. Then Finn moved on to the action Titch should take in the event of an emergency.

'It's important that you know how to escape from the mech in a hurry,' he said.

'You don't want to find yourself trapped if the machine takes a big hit.'

'You don't sound very confident about the next battle,' grinned Titch. 'But you might as well tell me. What do I need to know?'

The boys were standing at the top of the mech's steps, on the platform in front of the cockpit. Finn invited Titch to climb in.

'If you're ever in danger, LoneStar will instruct you to use the ejector seat.'

The on-board computer was clearly listening, because lights inside the cockpit started flashing.

'To eject,' it said, 'just press the button and hang on tight.'

'What happens?' asked Titch.

Finn was peering into the cockpit from the platform. He grinned mischievously.

'Just don't touch the button,' he said. 'Unless you're in big trouble!'

Next the boys turned their attention to the radar system. Finn wanted to make sure that Titch knew how to make full use of it. The device showed where his opponent was located on the battleground, but it could also reveal a lot more. Just as Finn instructed Titch how to activate the X-ray function, which would prove useful if a mech was hiding behind rocks, a roar of applause went up across the Armoury.

'What's going on?' asked Titch, climbing out of the cockpit to see for himself. He found Martha midway up the mech's steps, returning from the scavenger store. Like the boys, she too was drawn to the source of all the noise.

Titch peered across the Armoury. Every mech crew had turned to face the mouth of the canyon. As the recovery truck emerged, dragging the remains of a defeated contender, the victor strode out behind. Finn stepped beside Titch for a better look. He gasped when he saw the winning mech. Even Martha started shaking her head. Titch also recognised the robot. Its massive chrome tail was unmistakable.

'Scorpion!' whispered Titch, as the mech paused to bask in the glory of its win.

'So that's who you'll be fighting in the final round,' said Finn.

'Uh-oh,' said Martha, who continued up the steps to join them. 'That's not good at all!'

● ● ●

6

Breaking News

As Titch stood at the top of the steps, taking in the scene, he breathed out long and hard. Scorpion was one of the most feared mechs in the Battle Championship and Titch was well aware of the damage he could do to an opponent.

'It's the tail I have to watch out for,' he muttered under his breath. 'The tip is loaded with a computer virus. One strike can freeze the mech's system for several minutes.'

'If that happens,' warned Martha, 'it would be game over.'

'Good job you know how to use the ejector seat!' said Finn. 'When Scorpion closes in to finish off its prey, the end result isn't pretty. I've seen mechs that have been clawed and battered to bits.'

Titch didn't need any further explanation. The smoking remains of Scorpion's last opponent had just been delivered to its team. The pilot and his engineer were standing before the heap of tangled metal, looking very sorry for themselves.

Titch turned to Martha. 'So what weapons did you choose from the scavenger store?' he asked.

'The delivery will be here at any moment,' she said. 'Why don't you two grab some lunch while I bolt everything on? Bring me back a sandwich and I'll explain everything. By then LoneStar will be armed and dangerous!

Every Battle Championship always drew a massive crowd. As a result, the officials made sure that the mech crews had a secure place they could go to relax without being mobbed by fans. Showing their identity badges to the security team, Titch and Finn headed for the canteen. They took their meals to an outside table and sat down. A giant TV screen was showing replays of the morning's battle rounds. When Scorpion's round came on, the boys stopped munching on their sandwiches and watched closely.

'That machine strikes fast,' muttered Finn. 'It must have supercharged motors in its tail base. All we can hope is that the pilot makes it quick.'

Titch glanced across at his friend. 'You worry too much!' he laughed. 'It's going to be tough, but we're not beaten yet!'

On the screen, Scorpion's opponent had just been struck. It struggled to move, and simply quivered on the spot. But just as Scorpion prepared to pounce, the picture cut out. A moment later, a newsflash came on to the screen.

'We interrupt coverage of the latest rounds to report that a party of young Battle Championship fans have become trapped following a rockfall inside a disused gold mine. A rescue effort is under way, but the situation is serious.'

Finn and Titch looked at one another.

'It must be those guys we saw in the canyon this morning,' gasped Finn with a start. 'I hope they're going to be OK!'

The screen showed live footage from the entrance to the gold mine. It was clear that the falling rock had completely blocked any way in or out. A small group of rescue workers were lining up a drill, but it looked like they were struggling.

'A mech could clear that in minutes,' Titch said, standing up and pointing at the screen. 'We have to help.'

'But what about your final round?' Finn reminded him. 'I really don't think we'd get there and back in time. And you can't afford to miss it!'

Titch looked around. He spotted Alexei at a table, and hurried over to speak to him.

'You've seen what happened!' he said. 'Can't you take your mech out there? Your weekend is over after all!'

Alexei shifted uncomfortably in his chair. 'My mech's in for repairs,' he said weakly. 'I wouldn't want to annoy my mechanic by taking it away.'

'But this is an emergency, Alexei!' Titch frowned at his excuse. He glanced back at the screen. If his father had been faced with a situation like this, he thought to himself, what would he have done?

'We've got to go,' he said to Finn after a moment. 'I'm going to offer my help. Those kids are more important than a win.'

Finn looked torn for a moment. Then he hurried close behind.

•

Titch and Finn found Martha admiring the massive crossbow she'd strapped across the back of LoneStar, along with a belt of steel darts.

'That,' she said, pointing proudly at the weapon, 'is powerful enough to penetrate rock. What's more, each dart contains a zipwire that uncoils when fired. 'It could be useful to get from one canyon wall to the other if you choose to fight from up high. I've also bolted on a surge gun to each arm. They pack quite a punch. You could knock a mech off its metal feet using one of those.'

'There's no time for that now,' said Titch breathlessly, before explaining what had happened. 'If we hurry, there's a chance we can help with the rescue effort at the gold mine and make it back in time!'

'You're crazy,' said Martha. 'Even if your heart is in the right place.'

'So are you with me or not?' asked Titch.

Martha sighed to herself before taking a deep breath. 'All right, I'm with you. I don't believe we'll make it back for the final round, but as it's a matter of life or death, let's saddle up the horses and get going!'

'That'll take too long,' said Titch. 'We'll have to hitch a ride on LoneStar!'

•

With Finn at the controls, and Titch and Martha on the platform outside the cockpit, the journey through the canyon pass took over an hour. Titch and Martha gripped the handrail tightly. Looking out from such a height was scary stuff. The wind blew much stronger up above, while the movement of the mech left them both feeling like they were in the crow's nest of a ship on a stormy sea.

'I really hope we're not too late,' said Titch.

As the mech steered round a turn in the canyon, the scene of the accident came into view. Immediately, it was clear that the rescue workers hadn't made much progress with the drill.

'Those poor kids,' said Martha, as Finn stopped the mech and dropped the steps into place.

● ● ●

7

Emergency Rescue

Titch was first to race down to ground level. 'What can we do?' he asked the chief rescue worker, yelling over the noise of the drill.

The man ordered his team to shut off the machine so they could speak. He removed his hard hat and wiped the sweat from his brow. 'Do you think you can clear all this rubble with that thing?' he asked, and gestured at LoneStar.

'I'll give it my best shot,' said Titch before turning to scramble back into the cockpit.

With Martha and Finn standing aside with the rescue team, Titch guided the mech towards the rubble.

'This is more important than all the fights you've ever faced,' he told LoneStar. 'If there's any trick up your sleeve that can help, now would be a good time to let me know.'

'Let me check the database,' replied the on-board computer.

Titch watched the systems display race through a list of codes. Then, without warning or guidance, the mech extended the surge gun barrels from its wrists and fired at the rubble.

'Whoa!' cried Titch as the explosion caused the rescue workers to flee for cover along with the twins. 'Since when could a mech shoot without the pilot pulling the trigger?'

'You instructed me to pull a trick out of my sleeve,' replied LoneStar. 'I simply obeyed your command!'

'I didn't mean literally!' muttered Titch,

straightening up in the pilot's seat. 'Anyway, we can't just fire at will. There are people out there!'

'All mechs are programmed never to fire at humans,' the on-board computer replied, but Titch was less than impressed.

'Someone could still get hurt,' he said, and grabbed the control sticks. 'Now let's just focus on clearing these rocks.'

The mech made light work of the rubble. With Titch guiding the metal monster, it scooped away the blockage in a matter of minutes. The final rock proved the hardest to shift. It was lodged inside the mouth of the gold mine.

'There is another way we can clear this,' said LoneStar as Titch tried and failed to smash it away with the mech's hand curled into a fist.

'You're about to suggest we use the surge gun again, aren't you?' Titch sighed to himself. 'OK, but first let me warn everyone to take cover.'

Having addressed the rescue team through the loudspeaker system, Titch steered the mech backwards a step and took aim.

'Allow me to handle this,' said LoneStar. 'I'll activate the target precision locks to make sure that nobody on the other side comes to any harm.'

'I hope you're right,' said Titch, bracing himself for the recoil.

The shot rang out through the canyon. When the smoke cleared, Titch was overjoyed to see that the mouth of the gold mine was no longer blocked. What's more, he could just about see the young Championship fans jumping for joy.

'Powering up the orb lamps,' said LoneStar, upon which the tunnel was flooded with light from the mech's eyes. 'Uh-oh!'

Titch didn't need to ask to know what the problem was. In the light, it was clear that along with the rockfall, a chasm had opened up in the floor of the tunnel. It was basically a big drop between the mouth of the gold mine and the school kids. Without a doubt, it was too wide for them to jump. Just then, Titch's earpiece crackled, and Martha came online.

'This must have been caused by all that dynamiting. It's weakened the rocks. From where we're standing, we can hear the walls of the canyon creaking. We really need to get them out in case the whole mine collapses!'

Titch thought hard about his next move. The tunnel was too small for the mech to crawl through. Then he remembered the weapon that Martha had fitted for the final round.

'Listen up,' he said through the loudspeaker, addressing the group leader and the schoolchildren. 'I want you all to step back as far as you can. I have an idea.'

'What's the plan?' asked LoneStar.

'Arm the crossbow,' Titch instructed the on-board computer. 'But let me do the shooting, OK?'

A moment later, the mech was crouched on one knee before the mouth of the gold mine. LoneStar was brandishing the crossbow. The steel dart was locked and loaded.

'Be very careful!' LoneStar warned him.

Titch didn't reply. He was completely focused on the task ahead. Inching his control sticks to aim the crossbow, he targeted the wall of the gold mine on the far side of the chasm and fired. Whoosh! The dart shot into the mine, uncoiling the zipwire at a furious pace. Much to Titch's relief, it hit the target spot on.

'OK, let's tighten up that wire,' he said, and moved the mech back several steps. With his rescue plan in place, Titch snapped out of his seat belt and climbed out on to the platform.

'What are you doing?' Finn yelled as the rescue workers rushed to the mouth of the tunnel.

Titch responded by climbing over the platform and dropping down on to the shaft of the huge crossbow. From there, with his arms spread wide for balance, he made his way to the end of the weapon. Having reached the very end, he crouched down and swung on to the zipwire.

'I'm going to get them out of there,' he shouted down, moving arm over arm into the gold mine. It didn't take long to reach the chasm, which was where he focused hardest of all on reaching the other side. The slightest slip of his grip on the cable would've seen him plummet into what looked to Titch like a bottomless pit. Finally, he dropped to the floor to be surrounded by the cheering Championship fans.

'Listen up, everyone!' said the group leader, who had worked out the plan for herself. 'You need to copy what Titch has just done. Grab the cable with both hands and climb across to the other side.'

A gasp went up among the group. At the same time, a low rumbling sound could be heard within the rock.

'We need to go now,' urged Titch, helping the first person on to the cable.

95

One by one, they crossed the chasm. It was a heart-stopping moment for everyone involved. The rescue party had gathered at the mouth of the gold mine, along with Martha and Finn. They helped each person to safety on the other side, as well as the group leader when she crossed. Finally, just one girl was left with Titch on the other side. She looked terrified.

'I can't do it!' she whispered with tears in her eyes.

'We have no choice,' Titch urged her as another rumble loosened some rock over their heads. 'If we don't get out of here, we could be crushed!'

The girl didn't move. She was rooted to the spot with fear. It left Titch with no choice. As the others yelled at the pair to make a move, he reached up for the cable and then instructed the girl to wrap her arms round his waist. She shook her head furiously. Then a wooden roof support crashed to the floor behind her. It was enough to persuade her to take up Titch's offer. With the girl clinging on tight, Titch set out on the return journey across the chasm.

'Make it fast!' Martha called across. 'Any moment now it's going to start raining rocks!'

Titch was halfway across when the wall behind him began to crumble. He glanced back. It looked like the steel dart was about to shake free. Already, rocks were beginning to shake from the roof and drop into the chasm below.

'Keep going!' yelled Finn. 'Go, Titch. Go!'

Some of the rescue team reached out as Titch inched closer. He was almost there when the wall gave way completely. As the cable went slack, and the girl screamed, Titch grabbed the hand of the chief rescuer. With the pair dangling, other rescuers quickly rushed to the edge and helped to haul them to safety.

'That was too close for comfort,' cried Titch as the girl ran into her friends' embrace.

'We need to get out of here,' Finn said, looking up and around. 'This place is totally unsafe.'

Hurriedly, everyone headed for the mouth of the tunnel. As they surged out into the sunshine, the rumbling sound behind them turned to a roar. Titch spun around to see dust billowing from the gold mine as the passage collapsed completely. Just then, he realised with a jolt how close they'd come to a total tragedy. Titch felt shaken at the very thought, and took a few breaths to calm down.

'You did a fine job,' said the chief rescuer, coming over to clap him on the back. 'Without you, this would've been a disaster!'

'It certainly will be unless we hit the trail for Rust Town,' said Finn, who tugged at Titch's sleeve.

'The final round of this weekend's Battle Championship,' Martha added as if Titch could have forgotten!

'Let's get going,' said Titch, before turning to the mech. 'At least I've had some practice with the crossbow!'

● ● ●

8
Showdown

Before they'd even reached the canyon, Titch could hear the crowd. It wasn't cheering that reached his ears, as Finn was first to point out, but slow handclaps and booing.

'The final round has just started,' said Martha as the mech paced towards the battleground. 'People must think we've run scared.'

'Then we need to prove them wrong!' said Titch, before asking Finn to bring the machine to a halt.

'Get yourself into the cockpit,' Finn told him, scrambling out before rushing down the steps with Martha. 'Show them what you can do!'

Quickly, Titch strapped himself in. He pulled down hard on the control sticks and made his way to the battleground. As he did so, a red dot appeared on the cockpit radar.

'There's your opponent,' reported LoneStar. 'Another minute and Scorpion will be awarded an automatic victory.'

'Then let's make a surprise appearance!' said Titch, pushing the control sticks forward by another notch. It caused the great mech to break into a sprint with every footstep stamping a mark into the ground. The sound of pistons pumping echoed across the canyon, but even that couldn't match the noise from the grandstands. When Titch and his mech finally appeared, the audience responded with gasps and then silence. Inside the cockpit, Titch caught his breath when his opponent turned around.

'Heads up, Titch!' said LoneStar. 'Someone doesn't look very pleased to see you.'

Scorpion had clearly been preparing to celebrate. As well as the giant tail, curled high over its head, the machine possessed two enormous mechanical pincers. On seeing Titch's mech, it rose up on its hind legs and snapped both pincers menacingly. It sounded like swords clashing.

'OK, let's prime both surge gun barrels,' said Titch calmly. His heart was hammering, but he knew how important it was to stay focused. Scorpion prowled closer, flexing its tail at the same time, preparing to strike.

'Ready,' confirmed LoneStar.

'Let's do it!' Titch pulled the trigger and watched as the two guns unloaded their ammunition. Both hit the target dead-on in an explosion of fire.

'Bullseye!' cried the on-board computer. 'That has to be the winning shot!'

Titch didn't take his eyes off the screen. He waited for the smoke to clear, and then his heart sank. Scorpion appeared to have suffered no damage whatsoever. In fact, it remained in the same threatening pose as it had before Titch had pulled the trigger. The only difference was that its red eyes were glowing brighter than ever before.

'We have a problem,' said Titch, who then threw his mech to one side as his opponent sprang towards him. Scorpion landed on its pincers. The machine then flung the tip of its tail right over its head and into the ground where LoneStar had just been standing. 'Oh, boy, we're in big trouble!'

Titch scrambled the mech back on to its feet, narrowly missing a second strike. With no chance to gather his thoughts, he swung a fist at Scorpion. His opponent reacted with lightning speed and grabbed the mech's arm in one pincer. Before Titch could struggle to get free, Scorpion twisted around and hurled Titch's mech into the air. It did so with such force that LoneStar sailed into the air like a rag doll. Inside the tumbling mech, Titch was powerless to do anything but prepare for another hard landing. With a great crash, the mech hit the wall of the canyon and then slid into a heap on the floor. At once, several alarms started to ring inside the cockpit.

'Reporting damage to the hydraulic mobility network,' said the on-board computer.

'What does that mean?' asked Titch, who was trying desperately to get the machine to stand.

'It means we're not walking out of here,' reported LoneStar.

Across the canyon floor, Scorpion had

105

begun to advance towards Titch's mech. It lowered its head as it moved. Titch watched the machine's powerful shoulders bobbing up and down. Without thinking, he placed his thumb over the ejector seat button. Just as he prepared to press it, a thought crossed his mind.

'Is the crossbow still functioning?' he asked LoneStar.

In response, an image of the weapon appeared on one of the screens. It flicked from red to green.

'At least something's working,' muttered the on-board computer.

Titch guided the mech to hurriedly reach around for the crossbow. Before loading a dart, however, he grasped it with both hands. Then he bent the steel shaft.

'Don't ask me what I'm doing,' he told the on-board computer. 'Let's just hope it works.'

By now Scorpion was close enough to

cast a shadow over Titch's toppled mech. The machine rose up on its hind legs once more and, with a shriek, curled its tail high. Titch knew full well that he had just seconds to spare. Quickly, he aimed the crossbow not at his opponent, but slightly to one side, and then fired. Instead of leaving the crossbow in a straight line, the buckled dart, shaped like a boomerang, twisted into the air, dragging the zipwire with it. Scorpion wheeled around as the arrow spiralled past him, only for it come back full circle and promptly wrap round the mech. Within moments, Scorpion's arms and tail were tightly bound to its torso. The mech shrieked in fury, struggling to escape, and blowing several steam valves in all the effort.

'Finish him!' cried LoneStar. 'Hit him with a shot from the surge guns!'

Titch punched several buttons on the weapon selection panel. Then, with the

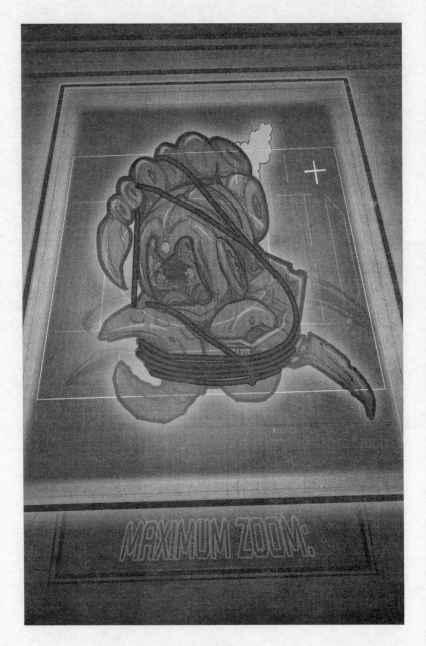

crossbow strapped across the machine's back once more, he took aim at Scorpion with both surge guns. Cross hairs appeared on the screen, which Titch steered towards his opponent's chest. By magnifying the picture, he could just about see the pilot through the glass of the cockpit hatch. He was still struggling to free his machine, but looked thoroughly defeated.

'There's no need to cause any more damage,' said Titch, switching off the cross hairs on the screen. 'Scorpion isn't going anywhere.'

Sure enough, a klaxon sounded just then. At the same time, the Battle Championship referee radioed in to confirm that the final round was over.

'You did it!' cried LoneStar. 'You've won maximum points from your first weekend on the Battle Championship trail. That's very impressive for a rookie like you!'

Titch could hear the roar of the

audience from the grandstands overlooking the canyon. It was hard to believe they were cheering for him. He looked up and saw that every single spectator was on their feet, clapping wildly.

'It's just a shame that LoneStar took such a beating,' he said.

'Martha will fix us up,' the on-board computer assured him. 'Now go and bask in your glory.'

It was LoneStar who released the locks on the cockpit hatch, only to sigh when they failed to move. Titch could see for himself that the hatch had buckled slightly from the impact with the canyon wall.

'Am I trapped?' he asked.

The on-board computer didn't reply for a moment. Instead, a series of numbers flashed on to the screen, before settling into a countdown from ten.

'Hold on to your seat,' said LoneStar. 'There's only one way out of here, and it's going to be quite a ride! Now get ready to press the ejector seat button!'

•

Martha and Finn had watched the whole fight from the grandstand. They had scrambled to find a seat just as soon as Titch and his mech set off into the battleground. Shortly afterwards, the group of fans they'd saved from the mineshaft arrived and took the seats behind them. They'd joined Martha in whooping with joy when Titch snatched victory from what seemed like certain defeat.

Now she and her brother stood open-mouthed as Titch was fired high into the air by the mech's ejector seat mechanism. Just as it looked as if he might crash back to the ground, the parachute opened up. Together, the twins watched Titch floating gracefully to earth and joined in with the cheers and whistles all around them.

'What a win!' cried Finn. 'Can you believe we're top of the leader board?'

'It took teamwork,' said Martha as Titch touched down. 'And what better way to end the weekend than with a first-round victory!'

• • •

9

Game On!

The celebrations lasted all afternoon. Titch could barely believe it when so many famous mech pilots stepped over to congratulate him. When the big screen showed the Battle Championship leader board, there was his name at the very top! His victory only really sank in when he stood on the podium to receive the trophy and the prize money.

'Half of that belongs to me, young man!'

Titch looked down at the crowd who had come to see him accept the trophy. A figure had just pushed through to the front. She wore an eyepatch and was

grinning broadly. Titch recognised the scavenger storekeeper straight away. He also remembered the deal that they'd struck.

'I hadn't forgotten you,' he grinned, before handing over half the wad of cash he'd just been presented with. 'Without your weapons, we wouldn't have stood a chance. It turned out to be a good deal!'

The woman slipped the money inside her pocket.

'Just don't let this moment go to your head,' she warned. 'You've made your mark here, but mechs will be all the more determined to defeat you at every battleground on the Championship trail.'

'I know that,' said Titch. 'I'll just have to be on my guard.'

The storekeeper studied Titch carefully.

'You remind me of someone who passed through Rust Town several seasons ago, you know. Another pilot, if I remember rightly.'

Titch's eyes opened wide. 'My dad was a Championship contender,' he told her. 'He went missing on the trail. I'm hoping to find out what happened to him.'

The storekeeper looked closely at him. 'That man was a legend,' she said eventually. 'You should be very proud to be his son. Now I think about it, he had the same crazy determination as you . . . the same fire in his heart when it came to piloting mechs. Such a tragedy that he never made it to the next round.'

'What do you know?' asked Titch in a whisper.

The storekeeper seemed to check her memory. Then she just shrugged. 'All I can say is that the trail from here is very dangerous. Badlands lie beyond the canyons. Bandits are known to roam in gangs out there. Some will do anything to lay their hands on a Battle Championship mech. The officials were right to forbid travelling after dark. That law came into force after your father went missing.'

Titch looked to the ground. He had heard enough. 'I refuse to believe that my dad has gone for good,' he said quietly.

The storekeeper nodded as if she understood, before melting away into the crowd. As she left, Martha and Finn squeezed their way through to join Titch.

'What did she have to say?' asked Finn, glancing over his shoulder.

'Oh, nothing really,' Titch shrugged. He couldn't explain it, but for some reason he didn't want to share what he'd just found out about his father. Instead, he preferred to hold on to the little shred of information for himself. 'She was just wishing me good luck for the rest of the season,' he said. 'So how is LoneStar?'

'Take a look for yourself,' said Martha,

inviting him to turn his attention to the recovery truck. It was just making its way back from the canyon, dragging not one fallen mech but two. Scorpion was still tightly bound in the zipwire, and would require cutting free. As for Titch's mech . . . well, it was clear to Titch that the machine had taken quite a beating, too.

'Leave it in my hands,' Martha assured him. 'LoneStar will be working with me to make sure that when we ride out, our mech will be in better shape than ever. What's more, we've earned a weapon we can swap at the next round. We might not need a crossbow where we're going, but every scavenger store on the trail will gladly trade it for something more suitable.'

Titch nodded and looked around. Already some of the teams had packed up and were preparing to set off. Alexei was just climbing into the cockpit of his mech. Titch called out his name to grab his attention.

'Can't stop,' Alexei called back. 'I heard that there aren't too many good places to stay at the next battleground, and I've no plans on sleeping under the stars. But hey, take your time, guys! Someone needs to serve as alligator bait!'

The twins swapped glances.

'Huh?' Finn looked completely puzzled and a little bit scared. 'Nobody said there'd be alligators on the Battle Championship trail!'

'Let's not freak out now,' said Martha, 'though he might be right because I do know where we're heading . . .'

As she spoke, Finn closed the cockpit hatch and fired up his mech. The three friends watched Alexei's machine stride away, followed on horseback by his mechanic.

'Swamplands,' said Titch, who had just worked it out for himself. 'One of the most dangerous destinations on the trail.'

Martha nodded. 'It's going to be an epic round,' she said. 'The battleground is thick with mist, tangled trees, creeks and—'

'Alligators,' said Finn, interrupting his sister. 'I hate alligators.'

'Then I'd better work fast on mending our mech,' said Martha. 'Clearly, it's important that we get there before all the rooms fill up!'

Titch smiled to himself. It was a thrill to have won this first weekend in the Championship, but an even bigger thrill to be in a team with two such good friends.

'Whatever the next round has in store for us,' he said, 'we'll face it together. If we stand a chance of becoming Battle Champions this season, it's vital that we keep working as a team!'

'Wise words,' said Finn, as the three headed back towards their mech. 'Unless we're forced to sleep round a campfire at the next round, of course,' he added.

'Because if an alligator comes creeping into camp, you know I'll be right behind you guys!'

Titch looked across at Finn, who snorted with laughter. Then he glanced up at his mech. It was clear that LoneStar was listening because the two red lights behind the visor lit up and then tightened, as if the machine itself was chuckling.

'I know that I can count on you all,' said Titch. 'When it comes to facing danger on this Championship trail, we'll look out for each other!'

● ● ●

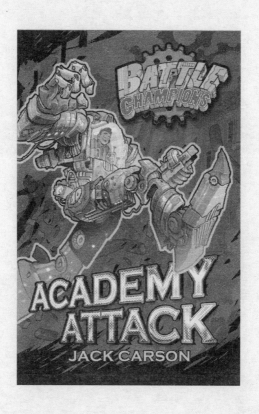

Titch Darwin has always dreamed of being a Battle Champion, but life at the world-famous Mech Academy is not as easy as it seems.

Read Titch's first mech adventure in Academy Attack!